THE BELLS OF CHRISTMAS

VIRGINIA HAMILTON

ILLUSTRATIONS BY
LAMBERT DAVIS

Harcourt Brace & Company
SAN DIEGO   NEW YORK   LONDON

First Harcourt Brace paperback edition 1997

Library of Congress Cataloging-in-Publication Data
Hamilton, Virginia.
The bells of Christmas/by Virginia Hamilton; illustrated by Lambert Davis.
p. cm.
Summary: Twelve-year-old Jason describes the wonderful Christmas of
1890 that he and his family celebrate in their home in Springfield, Ohio.
ISBN 0-15-206450-8
ISBN 0-15-201550-7 pb
[1. Christmas—Fiction. 2. Family life—Fiction. 3. Ohio—Fiction.]
I. Davis, Lambert, ill. II. Title.
PZ7.H18280n   1989
[Fic]—dc19   89-7468

E F D

Printed in Singapore

For wide-eyed children everywhere   —V. H.

Peace on earth, and good will toward all people   —L. D.

CHRISTMAS
1890

Mama Stringing Popcorn for the Tree

ONE

"Christmas comes but once a year," Mama said, eyes shining at me. "Only two more days!"

Christmas *never* comes when you are twelve, was what I thought. Each day was as long as a month. And the closer Christmas came, the more *never* it felt to me, even when I sat at my special place along the National Road.

"I want Uncle Levi and Aunt Etta Bell to *be* here," I said to Mama. And I want snow! I thought.

"Be patient, Jason," she said.

"I know who he waits for," piped my sister, Melissy.

"Lissy, com-bissy, tee-aligo-issy, tee-legged, tie-legged, bow-legged Lissy," I mocked.

"Jason, cum-bayson, tee-aligo-layson . . ." Lissy jeered back.

"That will be enough, you two," Mama said. "Here, take these lengths of popcorn and trim the evergreen. You'll make the tree look grand for Christmas Eve."

"I know. You're waiting for cousin Tisha," whispered Lissy.

"Hush!" I said it loudly, so Mama would know Lissy was a bother.

"Jason, try to get along," said Mama. "It's Christmas."

"No, it's *not*," I said, chin on my chest. "It's *never* Christmas. It's only Tuesday."

But I did wait for Tisha; we would have fun if it snowed deep. And I waited for Uncle Levi, too. Tisha hinted he was bringing a secret surprise for Papa. Wonder what it could be?

"I-can't-wait-for-Chri-isst-mas," Lissy started sing-songing. "*CHRISTMAS IS COMING!*" she boomed. "*THE GEESE ARE GETTING FAT. PLEASE TO PUT A PENNY IN AN OLD MAN'S HAT!*"

Her childish yelling hurt my ears. "Please, not so loud," I said.

She told me, "You don't have a piece to say at church on Christmas night."

"Pieces are for little ones like you," I said back.

"You will, too, do a piece, and right from the pulpit!" she shouted.

"What a pity to be Melissy and only seven at Christmastime. I'm almost grown up," I told her. "And you're not almost anything."

That quieted her for a moment. "Piece, piece," she said, "right from the pulpit."

"I'll have you know I'm singing a carol," I said. I couldn't help sticking out my chest. "Miss Perry told me I was to take the solo. 'Your voice has the purest tone and the sweetest tenor sound, Jason,' is what she said, right in front of everyone in our choir."

"Oh, sing it now, then, please?" asked Lissy, eyes shining just like Mama's.

"No, not now, Melissy. We have to decorate the tree."

Our Evergreen So Straight and Tall

Carefully we draped the long strands of popcorn over our palms and carried them like fine sheeting.

In the parlor we stood, staring. Some presents were there, wrapped and waiting under our Christmas tree. Up and up the tree went. It smelled winter green, bringing the outdoors in.

"It's as big as a house," said Lissy.

"That big," I said, "and it couldn't stand inside our parlor." But it was big. And ever green, I thought, ever so straight and tall.

So Tuesday went, with me trying not to fuss with my sister. She was a bother anyhow, and I was growing glum. The weather stayed fair yet cold, so cold I wore my wool muffler from morning till night. Outside, I stamped my feet to keep them warm. I wore two sets of knickers, and still I shivered all over.

"It's a time of admirable, clear weather," Papa said, from his rolling chair at morning table on Wednesday. Christmas Eve!

"Jason doesn't find it quite so admirable," Mama said, smiling.

No, I didn't, but I wasn't going to speak about it just then. I was eating eggs and ham, and hot milk sweetened with honey the way I liked it. I wetted cinnamon bread in the milk and slurped it all down. My older brother, Bob, was at table, too. He was the only one of my three brothers still at home. The other two, Ken and Samuel, were out of the house and married. But they worked each day with Papa as his carpenter's sure 'hands.'

"Doesn't look like it will snow," said Mama. "People can get around to do their Christmas shopping. And take their buggies on the National Road into Springfield-town." She poured strong black coffee for Papa.

"Everything will be ready for the Great Day," Papa told Lissy. He knew how she loved presents. I knew what she wanted and what Papa made for her. *I* wished for something rolling, but not like Papa's chair. Something that steamed and chugged. I didn't tell anyone because I knew things were costly. But if there were a *real* Santa, he would know I loved anything good and fast, with wheels.

"Without snow, we'll miss friend Wendell Maybry," Mama said. "And

Breakfast at Morning Table

his horse and his snow shovel. That man can shovel the town's walkways before most families push back from supper."

"That's the truth," said Papa. "I saw him just yesterday carrying gifts to the needy, since there is no snow."

"How nice," said Mama.

"Nice or not, fair weather is the worst," I said. I pushed away my cup. Yet I felt good and full to start my day. And now I had something to tell.

"Papa," I began.

"What?"

"They found the cave of the robbers."

"What?" he asked, again.

"Matthew had a Xenia paper," I said. Matthew Lawson lived down the lane. He was my best friend, next to Tisha.

"The paper told all about the James and Younger Gang, how they were discovered," I went on. Jesse James was a famous robber.

"Discovered in a cave?" asked Papa.

"Discovered in a *cave?*" copied Lissy, trying to sound grown-up like Papa.

"I saw the Xenia paper myself," I told him. "A cave somewhere in Minnesota 'wherein the Younger and James Gang hid during raids,'" I recited. "''And at the same time, the mystery of the disappearance of the youngest of the James boys has been solved . . .'"

"You made that up!" piped Lissy.

I made her disappear without once looking at her. "'. . . his skeleton having been found in the sub-ter-ranean ren-dez-vous.'"

"You have a good memory!" Mama smiled proudly at me.

Lissy sulked. Smiling still, Mama took the time to pat her curly head.

"That last word means meeting place," said Papa, explaining 'rendez-vous.' "And the other one — subterranean — means underground."

"I know," I said. I knew because Matthew told me. He was already thirteen, but he was shorter than Tisha and me.

"I wouldn't take everything as truth that I read in the papers," Papa said. "Jesse James was shot and killed in Missouri eight years ago."

"Still," I said, "That cave could've been his 'rendezvous' place."

On it went all morning. It was so hard, waiting for the Bells to arrive.

No, not Christmas bells, but Uncle Levi Bell, Papa's brother, a fine-wood carver. He was even better at fine-wood work than Papa. Aunt Etta Bell, his wife, was a teacher—retired—and she was coming, too. Chester, the oldest Bell son, was coming, and cousin Sebella, and Anthony, also all grown, and Letitia Ann, who is my age—all call her Tisha.

Tisha and I have grown tall together. We seem to grow about the same each year. We will have birthdays in January—mine the 15th and hers the 20th. Imagine having birthdays so soon after Christmas and getting even more presents!

"We are lucky ducks," Tisha always said.

Little Lissy asked, "Why are you ducks?"

Our House, Built by My Great-Grandpa

Tisha said, "This child has no humor under her silly goose feathers."

Matthew said, "Your cousin Tisha is the oddest girl." Still, he called her *fas-ci-nating* and vowed he would marry her one day.

I wrote often to Tisha where she lived near West Liberty, Ohio. She wrote me back, right on the National Road, Springfield. Our families traded Sunday visits once or twice a month. Then she and I would 'rendezvous.' We were tall friends always in touch.

My Special Place along the National Road

T W O

"Won't you wait outside with me, Papa?" I asked him that the first thing, early. He knew about my special place along the National Road.

"But your cousins won't be here for another day," he answered. "You will freeze if you wait that long." He winked at me.

"I can run in and out of the house to get warm," I told him. "Won't you please stay a little while by the Road with me?"

"We'll have to hurry a short visit, then," he said, while still at table. He winked again. Papa always winked. And looked the same as Uncle Levi.

He pushed back from the table in his chair on wheels.

"Can we ride the chair down to the Road?" I asked.

"Hurry, then," he said. "I must labor the morning if I'm to finish by tonight."

"Christmas is coming tomorrow, and the Bells!" I said.

"Yes," said Papa. "And your brothers and I have rooms of houses to fix yet today."

Papa went to fetch his peg leg. When he came from the bedroom, he walked on one true leg and the other, a wood peg. He pushed his wheel-a-chair before him. The wood peg he wore was the same length as his true leg from just above the knee down. It worked as well as the true right one. Papa always wore the peg leg to his labor.

I wished my papa had two true legs and feet. He never minded that he didn't.

"Been so long since I had two true legs and feet," he said once, "I've forgotten what it feels like. Doesn't matter atall. Peg leg made of wood is just as good."

Papa was a master carpenter, even with only one true leg. He made the woodwork for all the great houses of Springfield. He made cabinets, pantry cupboards, and fine tracery for windows and screens and panels. He taught the skill to Ken and Samuel. My brother Bob never cared for carpentry. He planned for college to become a teacher like Aunt Etta Bell.

Papa said that soon he and Ken and Samuel would form a company with hired laborers and work wagons and work orders. They would all be their own bosses, Papa said. Already there was a sign above the barn.

Mama was her own boss, a seamstress. Her dress shop was a room in the rear of the house. We called the room The Light because sunshine made it glow all day long. I helped run the shirtwaists, just finished, and the leggings and knickerbockers to ladies' houses. I knew all the ladies. Mama carried the silks by wagon — all of the cushions, eiderdown quilts, and robes. They were tied neatly in bundles. Lissy went along with her as Mama's 'hand.'

"We are coming up in the world," said Mama, pleased to make ladies' walking suits for Christmas, and all for pay. She made knickers for boys, too.

Papa and Me in the Wheel-a-Chair

But for my jackets and knickerbockers, she didn't charge a penny!

I wore my old Norfolk coat over my knickers. Papa wore his woolen coat over heavy work trousers and his carpenter's apron. We had on our caps.

"Hurry," I told him.

He smiled, telling my brothers to get the tools ready and all-such needed for the labor. "Be back shortly," he told them.

I held Papa's lunch. We said good-bye to Mama and Lissy.

"Now don't stay long by the Road," Mama warned me.

I smiled and knew I would stay. So did Papa know. He winked at me again.

We went off, out of the house, and riding. I sat so close to Papa in the big wheel-a-chair.

We went by way of the lane past our house to the Road. I worked the chair wheels with Papa. It wasn't hard. It's not far through the bare maple trees along the lane that parallels the great Road.

We rolled. We took the gentle lane-cut down the hillside, and the Road got closer.

That old bumpy pike! Seeing it made me feel swell, as if I were about to greet an old friend of the family.

The National Road could be quiet. But when a freight wagon loaded with barrels of goods came rumbling by—oh, then! Drawn by four or six draft horses. Big, heavy wagon, covered. The Road then rumbled like a hungry giant awakened by its noisy stomach!

I laughed, just because. So did Papa. We rolled slowly and came to a stop right beside the Road, and waited. Not long, a light delivery wagon came along. A driver sat up high, hauling rope and twine. We waved. The driver held the reins in one hand and waved back with his whip. His two horses high-stepped it.

He called, "Merry Christmas!" The wagon wheels clanged and clattered. I loved the noise of them, the turning over-and-round of them!

"Merry Christmas!" Papa called.

I jumped from Papa's wheel-a-chair.

The National Road

"Mr. Santa Claus is coming! The dingdong *Bells* are coming!" was what I yelled.

The driver laughed merrily and waved again. His nose was red with cold! I watched him disappear around a bend in the Road. The last sounds I heard were his horses whinnying and a low wagon rumble. They died away, and all was silent again.

I ran back to Papa, and he said, "A century ago my pa came and settled here, where there was not yet a road. There was only my grandpa's cow path. Fifty years ago, they built the Road where the cow path had been. And when I was a boy, when I was twelve . . ."

". . . you saw the giant covered wagons!" I joined in. I knew the story by heart. It was a true story, and all the better for that.

"Covered wagons came along this road by the hundreds," Papa said.

How I loved to hear the story!

"Like nothing I ever saw in my life before or since," Papa went on.

"Did they, Papa?" I faced him, my elbows on the chair rests.

Papa nodded, eager to remember. "This National Road was to be the first overland link between the Atlantic coast and the new state of Ohio. The covered wagons were called Conestogas. But only once in a while now will you see one hauling freight like in the old days."

I knew that trains now did the work of the Conestogas. But I didn't say it. I didn't tell Papa I admired the iron wheels of trains.

"Out west, the settlers called the covered wagons prairie schooners," I remembered. Matthew had told me so.

"Prairie schooners!" Papa exclaimed. "The tall ships of the Road. Some had wheels six feet high," he said.

Suddenly I remembered what I always forgot about the story. I didn't want to hear what would come next. Papa knew, and yet he went on a little more.

Quietly he said, "Accidents would happen, with so much traffic on the Road, and wheels that high."

"I know," I said. I managed not to look at his peg leg.

Wheels. I loved all wheels. I wanted to say, Let's talk about Christmas, about snowflakes, and a forever snow. But there was a pain between us like the quick prick of a needle.

I looked for clouds to speak about. The sky was an empty, winter-blue bowl.

"I've got to go now," Papa said. "Tell me you will be careful out here, Jason Bell."

"I am always careful, Papa." I sighed. Would Christmas never come?

Everyone told me to be careful. *You are the spit 'n' image of James Kenneth Bell, your father. Going to be a big, strong man just like him.* Everyone said it. *"So be careful."*

"Stay out of the way of the Road," Papa said. "And never walk in it to see one way or the other. Wait and listen. You have no reason to cross the Road."

Papa's Chair, beside the Barn

"I won't get in its way. I won't cross it," I told him.

He waved. We were only inches apart. He smiled. "Good-bye for now, Jason," he said.

"Bye, Papa," I said, and let go of the chair rests.

He rolled away to the barn. When he finished there, he would leave the chair outside. And I would fetch it back to home before snowfall covered it. Ah, me! I forgot. No snow! Just fair weather and cold. Gloom rested on me like a gray cloak.

My Brothers Samuel and Ken, Off to Labor

THREE

Papa settled himself in the top buggy drawn by the roan, Joe-easy. My brothers Samuel and Ken came over to drive the buckboard wagon full of tools and gear and ladders and such to the job. The horses, Samson and Delilah, lurched in their traces.

Papa's buggy glided away on the National Road. Samson and Delilah clip-clopped along, and the buckboard groaned and squeaked the way all wagons did.

Not far and Papa drew rein on Joe-easy to call to me, "Watch for a covered wagon, with Bells!" He laughed heartily at his joke — two kinds of bells. Bells that horses wear at Christmas. And Bells, my relatives. But a covered wagon?

"I know! I know! But not today!" was what I hollered loudly back. Then I heard my big brothers laugh. "Bye! All of you, bye!" was what I hollered last.

I longed to ride to labor with Papa. He said I could sometime when I'm thirteen. I'd go off to woodwork houses in what might well be Papa's own business by then — Bell & Sons. With a sign in gold words all across the front of the barn and the shed, too.

I stayed outside after Papa went to work. "Ring! Ring!" I sang softly to the air. Little gray puffs of my breath were like icy clouds out of my mouth. "You better hurry, Bells!"

I sat in the cattails next to the mile marker beside the National Road.

It was cold out there. Clear. Not a sign of a snow cloud in the sky over my house behind me.

Alone by the road, I sang, *"We live on the Road and go anywhere."* My voice was high and clear. *"The National Road. River of Central Ohio. Gone are the settlers rushing west. Gone is the mail coach, the ox-cart, the stage-coach, the covered wagon. But back then! Oh, then! Through Springfield to*

Indianapolis and on to St. Louis they went. Oh, the National Road!" I made up the song as I sang: *"Remember the wagoners with the Conestoga passenger ships, the stage drivers on gaudy coaches . . . and now, remember my papa and me!"*

I yelled my head off. I thought no one would hear me. But Matthew found me there.

"Heard your voice, so thought I'd come over," Matthew said. He'd finished his chores and could sit awhile with me.

"Was I that loud?" I asked, and then: "There's not going to be snow."

Matthew wrapped his arms around his legs. "We could go see if the pond is frozen," he said. "We could see if the geese have landed. They tell if there's to be snow."

Geese came ahead of the snow every Christmastime. Hundreds of them

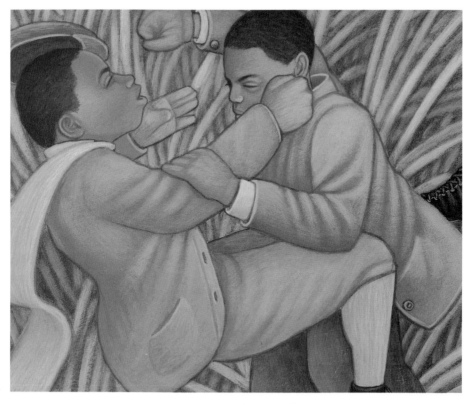

Matthew Got the Best of Me

to the pond there across the fields. Papa said when he was a boy, there were thousands of geese flying in flocks.

"Pond wasn't frozen yet on Friday," I told Matthew. "If it's frozen now, might not be thick enough with ice. I don't want to drown myself before Christmas."

"After Christmas, then," he said, joking, and changed the subject. "When are your relatives coming?" he asked.

"Who?" I said, teasing him. "Which relatives?"

He sighed. "The Bells from West Liberty, I mean," said Matthew.

"You mean Tisha, your great love! Ha, ha!"

He grabbed me, and we tumbled. We wrestled. He got the best of me, being already thirteen.

"Tisha loves another farm boy!" I hollered.

The words stunned him, and he broke his grip. "You take that back!" he shouted.

"Never take back the truth!" I said. "Matthew's love is stolen!"

Then it happened. His face was so angry. He *hit* me. He knocked me hard on my nose. I stared at Matthew, my friend — once. I never knew he cared so much for Tisha. Something dribbled down over my lips.

Matthew looked shocked. I took off my glove and wiped my mouth and chin. Wet red was on my palm. Then I felt the pain.

"You, Matthew! Take your hands off me!" I got to my feet. Blood, running onto my tongue. My nose hurt bad enough to bring tears to my eyes and a lump to my throat. Matthew looked afraid.

"I'm going home," I said. My voice was shaking.

"I didn't mean it, Jason," Matthew said. "Here." And he handed me his soft kerchief.

I took it, but it looked near new. I threw it back. I was hurt, and I wiped my bloody nose on my old Norfolk. "I'm going home."

"We could go to my house and have soup and crackers," Matthew said.

"No, thank you," I told him and turned away. Was this to be my merry Christmas?

Mama and Lissy, Dressmaking

"Jason, I didn't mean to hit you. But you tried to make me mad. And you did," said Matthew.

He was right. I was teasing. I slowed down to let him catch up. We walked single file through bare maples to my house. He followed me inside. We made no noise going into the kitchen. I filled the basin from the water reservoir in the stove. Mama and Lissy were in The Light, dressmaking. I heard the sewing machine whirring, powered foot-to-pedal.

I washed my face. Matthew helped me press the wet cloth on my nose until the bleeding stopped. We both sighed, glad no one had seen. We put the bloody cloth at the bottom of the coal bucket by the stove. It would get covered with coal dust — and hide the crime.

We sat on the front steps looking through the trees. I remembered to fetch Papa's wheel-a-chair from the barn into the house. Matthew helped me. Then we worked for Mama. Matthew stayed all day, helping, and watching over me. Finally we sat like gentlemen in the parlor. My nose no longer hurt. We talked about robbers and caves, snow and Christmas presents.

"Last year," said Matthew, "a man was playing Santa Claus and got too close to a gas jet."

"Is that so? And what happened to him?" I asked.

"His trappings took fire," said Matthew, "and it wasn't a second before he was wrapped in flames."

"No!" I said. Matthew nodded. We sat still among the growing shadows. We looked at the Christmas tree. Mama had placed a silk star covered with gold sequins at the very top. It shimmered there, as cold winter light from the windows touched it. Then the two of us thought and spoke on the lighter side of things.

"What do you suppose your Uncle Levi made me for Christmas?" Matthew asked. "Mama already placed the present under our tree."

Uncle Levi always made Matthew just the thing he wanted each year. "I know what it is, I think," I said. Toy soldiers of fine wood. "Tisha won't tell me, but she said I was getting warm." I smiled, but I didn't tell.

Matthew and I moved about, working on the tree. We hung brass bells and the tiny wood dolls Uncle Levi made for Mama years ago. They were so smoothly turned and painted all colors, with knickers and bustles. We took handfuls and hung them with care.

By evening, with everyone adding an ornament here and there, and the tree candles, the labor was finished.

Papa was home now and lighted the candles. Be careful! I thought. Don't get your trappings wrapped in flames!

"Oooh," cried Lissy, as the flickering lights made the ornaments glow.

Matthew stayed long enough to see how grand was our Christmas tree. I saw his the other day. It was sizable, but not so tall as ours.

Mama started a carol, and we sang of Bethlehem and the newborn king.

"Save the other carols for Christmas and my brother Bell," said Papa. He had taken off his peg leg. His trouser looked limp and empty.

"It's Christmas Eve Up Here Warming to Christmas"

"And all the other merry Bells," said Mama.

Matthew took a deep breath. I didn't tease him now.

"It's Christmas Eve! I don't believe it!" I said.

Papa laughed. Bob picked me up and hoisted me on his shoulders. Laughing, I touched the ceiling. "It's warmer up here, everybody," I told them.

"Is it Christmas Eve up there?" Bob asked.

"It's Christmas Eve up here warming to Christmas," I told him.

Mama's laughter tinkled like silver bells.

He set me down. "Christmas will come and go so fast, you will hardly feel it," Bob told me.

"I bet not!" I said. "I bet I'll know every minute of it."

Lissy Wondered How Mr. Santa Could Come down the "Chimley"

FOUR

"I'm going to stay awake for Santa Claus," said Melissy.

"Ah, no," said Bob. "Santa won't want you to lose your sleep."

"But I don't mind," she said.

"You'll be asleep by the time your head hits the pillow," I told her.

"Santa will come to my house first," Matthew said to me. "'Cause I'm the oldest. Merry Christmas, Bells!" He slipped out the door, leaving a blast of cold air behind.

"Merry Christmas, you bad boy!" Lissy hollered after him.

"Santa won't find you," I called. "You live too far down the lane. Merry Christmas!"

Melissy stood by the fire in the parlor. "Don't see how Mr. Santa can come down the chimley 'thout setting his britches afire. Will he be scarey-looking?"

"Don't you worry," Papa soothed. He gave her a ride on his wheel-a-chair. In the hall he gave her a circle ride. She squealed, "Wheeee!" Papa rode her to the stairs, and good night.

Christmas Eve.

"I don't believe it," I told my pillow, once I was in bed. I was both happy and sad. Happy that Christmas was almost to home. But no snow! Tisha wanted great mounds of snow. And then we would glide up and down the lane like grown folks, with me on one side of her and Matthew on the other.

"*Don't tell anyone*," her last letter had said. "*It's our pleasure, just the three of us. You and me and Matthew. I think he's a gentle and handsome boy, that Matthew, don't you? Don't tell!*"

I smiled into my pillow. And then in a wink, I was dreaming summer. Mr. Maybry planted snowballs with his shovel. Warm sunshine everywhere. His horse was made of Christmas chocolate and melted in the sun. Go-easy!

I dreamed I heard myself singing. My voice was loud like Lissy's.

Somewhere in the deep dark of night, when I slept the sleep of wishing and warm slumber, I dreamed I heard honking. Hundreds, honking. *"Ding! Ding! Dong! Jason Bell!"* It was as if the honking said that to me. I didn't quite know what it was. But merry! Merry Christmas!

And a long kind of tender ringing, like silver bells of Mama's voice singing, re-sounding and then quieting. Slowly, sweet slumber. The whole world, drowsy, adrift in the Santa Claus night.

I never knew how rested I felt until I woke up. I felt good. My room was light with a misty morning against the Jack Frost windows. Where did all that long night go?

Day. What Day? Did the Great Day pass by without me?

I leapt out of bed before I was all awake. I slid on the rag rug halfway to the door. "Wha—?!!"

I Smiled into My Pillow

Then I heard Lissy squeal. She heard me and came awake, too. She hit the floor, her feet scurrying. She came to me first, yelling my name in stair steps: "*Jason*-Jason, Jason, *Jason*-Jason . . ."

I met her, and we halted halfway down the up-stairs and I called, "Can we come down?"

"Can we, please, can we?" cried Melissy.

"Papa is just now working the fire," Mama called up.

The upstairs didn't seem quite so cold on Christmas Day. Still, Lissy and I shivered.

"I can't wait, Mama!" I hollered down. Brother Bob came to the landing still in his robe. "Christmas is down here . . . and all around here." He pretended surprise. "Don't know when it got here, but Santa sure emptied his pockets here."

"I missed him. I fell asleep. Let us come down!" shouted Melissy.

"Yes, let us, please. I can't stand it a minute longer!" I hollered.

"Well, then, if you don't run or jump the stairs, if you don't shout or scream . . ." Mama said.

We didn't let her finish. I shouted, "Merry Christmas!" Lissy screamed with joy. We jumped down and down. Brother Bob gave us a bow as we swept by him to the parlor. At the door, we halted and stared. I was holding Lissy's arm. She clutched my wrist. We couldn't move. We saw Papa, there at the side, smiling. Mama stood beside him. She was wearing a new dressing robe.

We saw just everything under the great tree. All that we wished was there. All the presents. And things we hadn't ever dreamed of.

"Well, come in," said Papa. "Looks like Santa loved this house, as did your Uncle Levi, too."

"Ah, no! It can't be," said I. For it was there, with wheels the same as real. A whole, splendid train on its tracks. Each train car painted in colors so fine and with lettering to say what it carried. A black engine and a fine caboose painted red. And so many wheels!

"It can't be, but it is!" It was all of wood made shiny, like iron. I sank before my train. I touched the smooth tracks with my fingers. I moved the

"Merry Christmas!"

engine forward, and all the cars followed, with a most wondrous clacking noise. Something went *ting, ting, ting, ting*. There was even a bell at the top of the engine. I shook my head. "I still can't believe it."

"Merry Christmas, son," said Papa. He looked as happy as I felt.

"It's just the best thing," I told him, my voice cracking. "But who . . . ?"

The train was made with strong, clear carving and fine working. The little raves on the sides of the cars were the kind Papa made for the sides of delivery wagons. Only these were lavish wood strips made tiny to fit. They were smooth and polished on my train cars. Some cars opened, and there were people sitting inside.

"Your Uncle Levi helped me with the delicate work," Papa said. "But I did all the rest."

"Thanks, Papa. It's the best train in the world!"

Then I was flat on the floor on my stomach. I remembered my manners soon, and attended to my other presents. Ah, so many things!

Under the tree was a new Norfolk jacket, my size. I took it and held it against me, so Mama would know I was proud to have it. "Oh, thank you, Mama. It feels warm."

"Welcome, Jason. Merry Christmas," said Mama. I unwrapped new knickers and button-up shoes for walking. I found jumping jacks, carved by Papa.

Melissy got a new frock and a pinafore with lace. White silk stockings—Mama made those. I saw I got a boughten Savoy suit to wear that day. Brother Bob got an Eton suit—he was grown up at eighteen.

And Mama got a fancy dress from Papa.

"Oh, James!" Mama said, pulling it from its box. "Oh, thank you, it's lovely!"

It had a bodice, close-fitting, tight, back-drawn skirts and a draped bustle effect, all in shades of blue!

Papa bought it for Mama because he admired the large mutton sleeves at the top, tight to the skin below the elbow. The fancy dress had a gorgeous muff to go with it.

The silk handkerchief I bought for Mama with my own money would go with it just swell. She said so, too, opening my present and laying it across the gorgeous muff.

"Thank you, Jason."

"Oh, we are going to be a sight at church this evening," Papa said, proudly holding his new suit up to his chest. He got a shaving mug and soap from me and Lissy. The mug had a painting of a carpenter and his hammer on it. And a tiepin with a pearl in it from Bob. And new carriage lamps from my oldest brothers.

Bob couldn't wait to try on his suit jacket over his night robe. It fit, but he looked so comical! I died laughing.

Melissy? Lissy? I saw her clothes, a muff, and the boa I bought her, too. But so busy was I with presents, I clean forgot about her. It was like voices

A Whole, Splendid Train on Its Tracks

of everybody got all mixed up in the gray light streaming in. No sunlight?

"What time is it?"

Mama laughed. I didn't say more. There was Melissy rounding the other side of the tree. Lissy?

"What?" I got to my feet. I went around there, greeted her as she came back to the front of the tree. Ah, me!

"Ah, Lissy! She's beautiful!" I said.

"You'll not find another one of them in these parts, I'll wager," said Papa.

Lissy didn't look up or say anything. Her eyes saw only what she held by the hand.

"She Walks . . . She Walks"

FIVE

"She walks . . . she walks," murmured Bob, smiling fondly at Lissy.

She was a doll the likes of which I'd never seen before. A walking doll dressed so fine. When Lissy walked around, holding her by the hand, the doll walked like a dressed-up lady.

"Uncle Levi made it for Lissy," said Mama.

"The design comes all the way from across the ocean," said Papa.

"She walks . . . she walks with me!" chanted Lissy.

She was somewhat stiff-walking, but perfect of face and limb. With arms and legs, a round face. With bright, dark eyes and a smiling mouth.

"Your Aunt Etta Bell hand-sewed the velvet dress with the bustle and the hat," said Mama.

"Santa Claus helped," said Papa. "He flew down the 'chimley' and walked the doll right to our Christmas tree."

"Ah, Lissy," I said, "your dolly walked in before all the Christmas Bells!" I knew Uncle Levi and Aunt Etta wanted her to have her present the first thing.

There was a humming sound inside the doll as she moved. I heard it when Papa said, "Shhh, listen." And she walked.

"A mechanical doll," said Bob. "Almost like she's human."

"A fine work of craft," said Mama. "I declare, she looks like Lissy's playmate and not a doll atall."

"Can I take her outside?" asked Lissy, coming out of her happy trance.

"Not this day," said Papa.

"I'll go with her," I offered. "We'll walk the lady doll over to Matthew's house. His whole family will want to see this."

"Not this day," said Bob, sounding just like Papa.

"Well, why?" I asked him.

"Well, just look out the window!" said Mama.

"Huh?" Lissy and I said together.

33

I was like a mechanical doll myself, going to the window. The curtains were closed. I was almost afraid to open them.

"Come, let's see," I heard Lissy say to her walking doll.

And, holding back the curtain, what I saw made my heart leap. "Ah, Lissy, look! Look!"

She looked. I heard her gasp. "Ah, me!" she cried.

"Snow! Beautiful snow!" I shouted. There is nothing like it when it falls in great sweeps that carry you up and up as you watch it fall.

"I don't believe it!" I said.

"Believe it," Bob said.

"The kind of snow that comes and goes . . . on and on," said Papa.

"You'll surely remember this deep snow of Christmas, 1890!" said Mama.

Snow, Beautiful Snow

"Oh! Oh!" I said. I rushed around the room. I had to get ready. "When will the Bells . . . I have to take a bath and get dressed! Mama, Papa, let's eat breakfast, the Bells will . . ."

"There's time enough," Mama said, "but we do need to get ourselves ready."

I was too excited to eat much breakfast. Time and again I left the table to see out the window. The brown, hard ground was gone 'neath the whitening. Every tree had its snow decorations. Our maples were dressed in white coat-ings. The snow made mist. It gathered the day in a soft-light mystery. There were no other boys in the world save for me. No cats and dogs, nothing, save the glowing snow, landing as I watched it fall. Oh, it was mine, this snow, 1890! I called it. I dreamed it.

"Papa!" I shouted and went back to table. "I must go see how deep the snow is on the National Road."

"Can I go, too?" cried Lissy. "Can me and my dolly go, too?"

You little baby! "Mama, make them stay to home," I pleaded. "It's my job to see."

"Well, the doll mustn't get wet," said Papa.

"Nor mustn't little girls," I said.

"Jason Bell, it's Christmas," Mama scolded me. "Where are your manners?"

My chin was on my chest again.

"The snow gets deep, probably a good three inches already, and drift-ing," Papa said. "Folks will soon be out and about, a-slipping and sliding."

He was worried about me near the Road.

"I'll take them both out," said Bob.

"That's good of you," said Mama. "Lissy, you hold Bob's hand. And Jason, you hold hers."

I swallowed and agreed.

Lissy looked happy, although she'd have loved taking her dolly out. "Next week on a dry day," Mama said.

Forever, it seemed, to get us all ready. Brother Bob first had to saddle

Bathing before the Woodburning Stove

Joe-easy and stamp out a track through the snow down the lane and to the Road and back. Then he attached a heavy sledge to Joe-easy's traces to work the trail into a smooth bed, wide enough for a buggy.

While that was going on, me and Lissy took turns taking our baths in the wood tub set in the kitchen before the woodburning stove. There was plenty of Christmas food cooking. Some, like pies and cakes, were already set and cooling, and waiting in the pantry. Me and Lissy went about our own business, and we were soon combed and polished. I wore my heavy coat and so did Lissy, with her hands warm in her muff. I had new gloves to wear and new hightop shoes. Mama stitched wool to them above the ankles to keep the snow out.

Then Bob was ready to take us down to the National Road. Not that I needed him to take me. But Lissy needed a sure hand.

"How nice you look," Bob said to us, as we came out.

"Thank you," I said. "You look nice, yourself."

He had freshened up and changed clothes. His high stiff collar with turned-back corners was as white as the snow. Over that was a wool scarf, and a knitted cardigan that Aunt Etta Bell had made him for Christmas. She did so well, Mama said, with the knitted designs. He wore his dark sack coat of smooth fabric and his new suit trousers worn in his boot tops. I thought my big brother was handsome to beat all. So did the older girls at church!

"Do we look like Santa has been visiting?" asked Lissy.

"Yes," said Bob. "You look like Santa sat himself down in the parlor and didn't want to leave."

And off we went to the Road, with Bob on one side of Lissy, and me on the other.

There was hardly a sound out, save our footfalls on the path. Snowflakes swept into our faces, taking our breath a moment. The snow fell all over us, so smooth and sweet-smelling to me. I took a deep breath and let it out slowly, I was so happy.

The tall maples in their white winter coats were soldiers guarding our way. Or ladies all dressed up and waiting for the dance.

Bob and I let Lissy loose once so she could make a snowball. She made a dainty one.

"Stand still while I hit you with it!" she told Bob.

"Don't do it, Bob!" I said. But he did it. He stood there, and she threw — too short. We all laughed. Lissy got a second chance. I helped her aim. This time, she gave Bob a good one, right on his arm.

Then we went on our way again. The closer we came to the Road, the more we could hear. Snow slapping like seeds thrown against snow already fallen. The air was so crisp I thought I could hear it snap. Not bitter or icy. But winter right and proud. Winter perfect is the way the air seemed to me.

"Snow's getting on my new clothes," said Lissy, pouting.

"Well, it's supposed to," said Bob. "That's the desire of snow, to get as close to you as it can."

Bob, Hit by Lissy's Snowball

We laughed and laughed at that.

Now we could hear the jingling from the Road.

"Lots of folks are outdoors before the holiday meal," said Bob.

"Is that so?" I asked.

"Yes, always so," Bob said.

"I don't remember a lot from one Christmas to the next," I told him. I couldn't help my voice sounding too high. I was *so* excited.

"I don't remember last year and last Christmas atall," said Lissy.

"That's 'cause you were so little," I told her. "But I bet you'll remember this one."

Teams of Horses Pulled Sleighs on the Road

SIX

Lissy smiled and looked happy as she could be. Well, it was Christmas, and to me it felt like she was less of a bother as the day wore on.

We broke out of the trees, away from the patches of cattails, and stood a few feet off the Road.

"Ah, me!" I exclaimed.

"Ah, me!" said copy-cat Lissy.

"That makes the three of us — ah, me!" said Bob.

All was a sight to see on this Great Day. On the National Road!

And bells. Bells! No, not my relative Bells, not yet!

But bells, sets of three or five attached to the collars around horses' necks. Sometimes there was a whole string of bells tied to horses' harnesses. As the horses of a team moved, guided by the driver holding the reins, the bells sounded *jing-jing, jing-a-ling!* up and down the Road. And *ching, ching-aling*.

"Never in my life!" said I.

"Never in my life!" said Lissy.

Bob laughed. "Then feast your eyes!" said he. "This is the best part of a deep-snow day."

The snow kept on snowing, all over us and everything. Horses, teams of two and four, pulled sleighs! And the sleighs were full of laughing, talking, shouting Christmas folks. Whole families sometimes, if a sleigh was large enough. Whole families out for a sleigh ride before the favorite, Great Day supper.

The sky emptied its heart out. I knew I would hear the scudding sound of sleigh runners gliding through snow even in my dreams. And the muffley clip-clop of teams as snow deepened on the Road.

"Bob, will our sleigh work — can we sleigh ride?" I asked.

"Yes! Yes!" shouted Melissy. "Let's go before the snow stops!"

The Bells Arrive

"This snow won't stop, Lissy, not for a good while," Bob said. "We'll sleigh ride when the relatives get here."

The snowfall and the sleigh bells must have heard him. For all at once there was a shout down the Road. We all turned as a four-horse team pulling a large, covered sleigh swung into view. The riders had spied me and Bob and Lissy before we spied them.

"Ho-ho!" shouted Bob.

"Ho-ho-ho-o-o!" came the return call.

"Bells!" I shouted. "It's Uncle Levi!"

"They're here!" shouted Lissy.

We jumped up and down for joy.

The horses came on, decorated with harness bells. They trotted briskly and snorted loudly at the driver's directions.

The covered sleigh top was homemade and fashioned to look like an old Conestoga wagon top.

Oh, it was a sight, that sleigh of merry Bells. "Tisha! Tisha!" we called out.

"You look like pioneers!" I hollered.

And they all waved and laughed and shouted, "Merry Christmas, Bells!"

"Same to you!" I called.

"Jason! Lissy! Bob! Jason! Jason! Merry Christmas!" called Tisha.

Then they were with us. Tisha was just the prettiest girl! She wore a hooded cloak of dark wool and a skirt with back drapery.

"You look all new!" I told her, gaping. "Haven't seen you in *so* long!"

"And you!" she said, eyes big and wide. "Jason, you look thirteen!"

Uncle Levi and Aunt Etta Bell gave hugs all around. The older brothers, Anthony and Chester, and cousin Sebella, took in Christmas packages.

The best gifts for the younger relatives had been exchanged. But there were some few gifts, such as Jason's from Tisha, and goods for the best meal, that had come with the Bells on this Great Day.

My present for Tisha was waiting for her under the tree.

"My pa has brought his grand surprise for Uncle James," whispered Tisha. "Remember, I said it was a secret, and I can't tell."

"Yes," I said. And I wondered all over again what it could be.

"You'll be surprised," she said.

Then brother Bob and Chester, my oldest Bell cousin, took Lissy, me, and Tisha for a sleigh ride. Just a short one. For the team was tired and needed tending to.

"Oh, now!" I said to Tisha. We were settled under the blanket, and we were a grand sight through the snow on our lane by the National Road. "How are you — shall we stop for Matthew?"

We did stop for him. We talked excitedly about everything as we neared his house. Tisha called from the sleigh: "Here, Matthew. I've come to get you!"

The door of Matthew's house flew open. Matthew sprang out so quickly he fairly slid halfway to us.

Jing-Jing, Jing-a-Ling!

"Ah, gee! A fine sleigh this is, is it new?" he asked, climbing in next to Tisha. I was on her other side. Lissy sat in the front seat between Bob and Chester, listening to their eager talk.

"Poor Matthew! I suppose you've forgotten me as well as this sleigh. Now then, shall we ride, or shall we take you back before you forget where you came from?" she asked.

Matthew sat grinning from ear to ear. But his tongue was tied. Speechless.

"We ride! We glide!" I said. Matthew stole glances at Tisha. She looked just perfect, I thought. I was proud she was my relative and here for the Great Day.

"Aunt Lou Rhetta made this wonderful cloak," Tisha was telling Matthew, about Mama. "There's no other like it," said Tisha.

"It looks so nice on you, too," said Matthew, shyly.

I smothered a laugh so as not to disturb their talk.

"And this muff my ma found for me. I put it to my face when my nose gets cold," said Tisha. "I declare, I no longer can feel my feet!"

Matthew looked ready to wrap her feet in the blanket and run to the fire with them.

I grinned and looked away. I knew Bob and Chester smiled as Lissy chattered about the snow making her a white cloak with a hood, like Tisha's.

Soon we headed back, and in no time we were home. The house was a supper house, full of smells of good food — a mixture of sauces and meats and desserts. The spicy-sweet scent of pumpkin pie rode high above everything. My big brothers Ken and Samuel were here now with their families. The house was just full to bursting with relatives. Tisha and I circled the tree. I gave her the present I had picked out for her.

"Oh!" she exclaimed. "I did hope for a toilet set!" It had a brush, a comb, and a mirror. "It's so pretty, thank you, Jason."

She gave me a pocketknife of quality, and I praised it highly and showed Matthew.

"That's the finest I've seen," he said. Shyly, he handed Tisha his gift for her.

"I adore presents at Christmas," she said, and opened it. It was a bracelet with charms upon it. Quite pretty, too, and Tisha was delighted.

"Matthew, you weren't to spend a great lot of money, don't you know," she told him. But I could tell Tisha was pleased. Matthew had saved for months.

Then he went home for his supper. I thought he might refuse altogether to leave Tisha's side. "You can come back for pie," she said.

"I will," said Matthew.

Oh, but Christmas lasted long on its Great Day! I was filling up with it, and each sweet morsel of it was the best yet.

Mama received wonderful bead necklaces from Aunt Etta. She presented Aunt Etta with a silk umbrella. Aunt Etta *loved* it. She and Tisha and I went outside to open it. We three got under the umbrella.

Matthew Gave Tisha a Gift

Large flakes of snow came streaming down upon it as we stood there, shivering.

Papa gave his brother, Uncle Levi, a spokeshave, a cutting tool with a blade set between two handles. Uncle Levi was pleased.

We all waited eagerly to see what Uncle Levi would give to Papa. But they took Papa's present and went into the sitting room. They were gone a short while. And in that time, we children helped out. We moved tables, spread tablecloths, and arranged chairs for supper. Tisha and I placed the plates and silverware.

Papa and Uncle Levi Entered the Parlor

SEVEN

When Papa and Uncle Levi made their appearance, we were all back in the parlor. Mama had herded us there to sing carols. We had finished a sweet "Silent Night" when in came Papa, empty-handed. I couldn't see the present. It had been wrapped in a big box, too. Uncle Levi didn't have it either. What had happened to it?

Everybody stared at the two of them. Papa cut quite a figure in his Christmas suit. As he walked toward all of us and the tree, he held onto Uncle Levi's shoulder.

"Well, I declare," said Aunt Etta Bell. "Lou Rhetta, it sure is a wonder!" And she smiled brightly at Mama and all around. Mama looked Papa up and down and then, she, too, broke into a smile. "It's a wonder, indeed!" she said.

"And takes some getting use to, I'll wager," said cousin Chester Bell.

My brother Bob nodded agreement. "Papa will get used to it as quick as you please, if I know him," he said.

Well, I wondered! I gazed at my papa and he looked just like my papa, which he was. It was Christmas, with everybody and Tisha and oh, so many new things and goings on. That was the wonder, that I could see anything atall.

"What in the world is everybody talking about?" I asked.

"Yes, what are you all talking . . ." Lissy began.

I cut her off. "Hush up!" I said. I did not like being left out of things.

Papa smiled at me and said, "Calm down, son." He took his hand from Uncle Levi's shoulder.

"Now," said Papa, "come see what your Uncle Levi made me."

There was silence as I came up close to Papa. Lissy was right behind me with her walking doll. Everybody else crowded around. To my surprise, Papa raised his pant leg.

"Just look," said Papa. "Two true feet!"

I bent near with my hands on my knees. Well, it was a shock! Sure enough, where once there had been only the tip of a peg leg, there was now a shoe. And I hadn't noticed atall. And in Papa's stocking in the shoe was a foot. It matched the foot he'd always had. Attached to the foot was an ankle and then a leg. Not a peg leg atall. It was a wonder, all right.

"Knock on it, Jason," said Papa. And I did. I knocked on the leg, and it was wood. Very gently, I touched it with my fingers, and it was smooth oak, turned and made perfect by a master carver. It looked true, like the one that was real.

I shook my head, it was so hard to believe. "Is it a mechanical thing?" I asked Uncle Levi, for I knew he had made it.

"In some ways it is," said he. "There are wonders going on in mechanics."

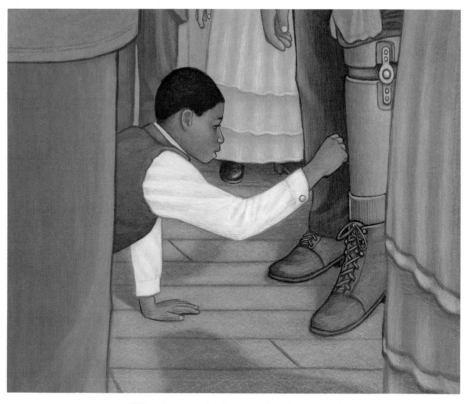

I Knocked on the Leg, and It Was Wood

"The foot moves up and down, like any foot," said Papa, "and it walks comfortable. For now, I will wear Levi's fine 'mechanical thing' on special occasions, such as this Great Day."

We all applauded wildly.

"You should both take a bow," said brother Bob. And they did. Uncle Levi and Papa bowed, holding onto each other for support. Each swept his free arm back in a grand gesture. They gave us a swell stage bow.

"It's a great wonder," I said, "to have a mechanical leg and foot. Papa, you look just like everybody!"

The grown-ups laughed at that. I was not too embarrassed. Tisha knew what I meant. So did Papa. It was a good son that wanted his papa to be just like folks. Oh, I liked him fine in his wheel-a-chair or on his peg leg. He was only different to me because he was such a fine carpenter and woodworker. But his two true feet did look the marvel. And then I just swelled up with pride at my papa and Uncle Levi.

"I'm glad of you both!" I couldn't help saying. "What true brothers you are!" And then Papa put his arm around me. And it was me and Uncle Levi who helped him to the dining room, and then into his wheel-a-chair, off his new leg for a while.

Well, it was a wonderful Christmas, 1890. A Great Day. The meal made our long supper table groan. Everybody talked and ate turkey and rabbit, sweet potatoes and turnips from our own root cellar, and hot bread and rolls and apple butter.

And, oh, that pumpkin pie! I could've cried, it tasted so good. Tisha said she could've died over it.

Well, that made Matthew laugh. He was back with us for the dessert. I gave him a spin top for Christmas, and he gave me the same! He gave Lissy a fine ball. And, besides the boa I gave her for dress-up, I gave her paper dolls with sets of paper clothes for play, which she loved. And Matthew got what he wanted from Uncle Levi, too. Matthew looked amazed when Tisha gave him what he would call ever after his *grand* muffler. It was long and striped, and Tisha knitted it herself. It looked comical draped around Matthew's thin neck. The fringed ends fell almost to his knees.

Supper on the Great Day

"It looks just right on you, Matthew," Tisha said, eyes shining.

"It does!" I agreed, chuckling out loud.

"What's so funny?" said little Lissy to a giggling Matthew. "What are all those stripes?"

And then we three—Matthew, Tisha, and me—*did* just about die laughing.

There was quiet talk, over coffee and chocolates made by Tisha and Aunt Etta. Everybody stayed close, leaning elbows on the table now as the table was cleared.

"Another Christmas," said Mama, happily.

"Another Christmas," said Uncle Levi, "and all of us, together."

"Still prosperous," said Aunt Etta, her face like sunshine.

"A hundred years of us Bells," said Papa, "who've lived long by the National Road. And this house," he added. "This house that Grandpa built."

"My great-grandpa Joshua Levi Bell," I said.

Uncle Levi nodded. "Grandpa was a drover along the Road out there. He and his helpers drove turkeys and sheep to market for landholders," Uncle Levi said. "East they went, a few miles each day. At nighttime, Grandpa rented pasture pens along the Road to keep the stock safe. He had some few of his own stock in there, too. Oh, it was quite a time, with thousands of head of animals in pens overnight, to be driven out on the Road by morning. And all kinds of easy transport—wagons, fast coaches, sleighs, sulkies all mixed in with the animals. And troops of immigrants, walking, driving cows and hogs . . ."

"And, did you know, Sherman and his army came eastward and passed along the Road after the Civil War?" Papa asked.

"No!" said Matthew and Tisha and I.

"No!" said Lissy.

"Good times and bad times," added Uncle Levi. "And all times of this family."

There was silence then at the table. Mama's cider was warmed and poured into glasses with cinnamon sticks, and we children loved the steam from it up our noses, and the taste.

Our Church

It wasn't ten minutes later that Mama said, "Goodness! Look at the time! The church!"

We scrambled then. All of us, rushing to fix ourselves up, then jumping into coats and hats, mufflers. For the entertainment at church on Christmas night was the height of it all.

"It's still snowing!" I yelled, surprised as I could be.

"It's never going to stop," said Tisha.

"Then you'll stay here forever!" whispered Matthew, just for her, but I overheard.

Outside, our sleigh was ready, pulled up behind Uncle Levi's Conestoga.

My older brothers had brought their own sleighs for their families.

"We're going to be a parade of Bells!" I hollered, and all the Bell fellows called, "Yes! Yes, indeed!"

"And Matthew!" cried Tisha.

And we all shouted, "Matthew, too! Matthew, too!"

The next thing and we paraded our sleighs down the lane, with all of our Christmas bells *ching-ching-chinging* in time with the horses' trotting.

Other sleighs, more and more of them, formed a great caravan on the National Road. Sleigh lanterns shone the way, showing how heavy was the snowfall. My brothers had fixed a calash, a folding top to our sleigh, but it didn't cover all of us in the front with Bob—Tisha and me and Matthew and his grand muffler, squeezed in tight.

Lissy was singing her head off in the back seat with Mama and Papa.

Well, we all joined in. We couldn't help it. It sounded like the whole National Road was singing. I hadn't thought about my solo once this day. I knew it well. But now I thought I would die if I forgot the words.

All else was a fog of falling snow, of gaslights shining like stars off in the city of Springfield, of churchbells ringing. The great crush of folks in our church. And children, dressed up and ready with their pieces—sayings and songs. Each child was given a sack of candies, fruits, and nuts. The ushers passed out the sacks from under the church Christmas tree.

Such a tree, with each family bringing it something nice. Our family had given bright, cotton balls that Mama covered in blue and pink silk. Our relatives gave wood deers with Santa and sleigh, all carved and painted red and green and white and black. All the children went up to fix their family decorations to the tree.

After the choir sang in praise, the entertainment began. Lissy went before me, and Tisha after me. Matthew got through his piece first:

"There's a star in the East on Christmas morn. Rise up Shepherd and follow." Matthew didn't like to sing so he said the words, and well, I thought. I clapped loudly for him; so did Lissy and Tisha, and Matthew's folks and his little brother.

Altogether, there were twenty pieces and songs as entertainment. Lissy surprised us all, except for Mama. It was her and Lissy's secret that Lissy would sing. I was struck dumb by the sound of her little voice, and she stayed in tune, too. With Miss Perry playing the piano for her and smiling.

Lissy Sang Her Piece

"Up on the housetop reindeer pause," Lissy sang. *"Out jumps good old Santa Claus. Down through the chimley with lots of toys. All for the little ones' Christmas joy."*

Well, we clapped and clapped when she was through. And I was as proud as I could be. She had stood so straight and tall by the piano, such a young lady.

When it was my turn, I strode to the piano next to Miss Perry. I held my head high, and did not look at the other piece-sayers in the front pew for fear the boys my age would make me laugh. I let my voice sail out over the congregation:

"We three kings of Orient are. Bearing gifts we traverse afar. Field and fountain, moor and mountain, following yonder star."

When I came to the chorus, I lifted my voice up to my highest tenor sound:

"Oh, star of wonder, star of night. Star with royal beauty bright. Westward leading, still proceeding. Guide us to thy perfect light . . ."

My voice echoed off the walls and stained-glass windows. When I finished finally, the sound of my voice still rang. I looked at my family. Mama and Papa, Uncle Levi and Aunt Etta—they were just so still, eyes misty, that I had to look down. Then, the clapping swelled. I put my hands deep in my pockets. For the applause caused a rush of caring in me for everyone present. I grew shy and my face, hot. Finally, I had sense enough to sit down right by my best friends, Tisha and Matthew.

It was Tisha who ended the entertainment.

"Children, listen," said our minister, Reverend Brandwell. "Miss Tisha Bell will say her piece now, bringing our splendid evening to a close."

And it didn't matter that what she said had already happened. We all loved it and knew it would happen again next year:

"'Twas the night before Christmas, when all through the house
Not a creature was stirring, not even a mouse . . ."

Oh, it was a long poem, and she didn't forget a single word:

"—And giving a nod, up the chimney he rose.
He sprang to his sleigh, to the team gave a whistle,

And away they all flew, like the down of a thistle,
But I heard him exclaim, ere he drove out of sight,
'Happy Christmas to all, and to all a good night!'"

We went home with sleigh bells ringing. This time, I was back with Mama and Papa and let Lissy bother Tisha and Matthew in front with Bob. I was in the middle and warm as I could be. Tired I was as I rested against Papa's shoulder. "It has been a great day," I said.

"It always is," said he.

"For the last hundred years, you think?" I asked.

"It's been a great day, from then at least," he said, "through good times and bad."

"Do you think a hundred years from now," I began, "children and their folks will ride their sleighs down this National Road on Christmas night?"

Sleighing toward a New Century

"They'll be on this road a good long while," said Papa. "But I heard tell of horseless carriages across the ocean. There was one driven by steam that had three wheels. I don't doubt there will be horseless sleighs one day as well."

"No!" I said. "A horseless sleigh! A horseless carriage! I wish I could be around for that!"

Papa and Mama laughed. "I think you'll have your chance," said Papa, "for a new, twentieth century is just up ahead."

"Oh, very good!" I said as I snuggled down.

Lo and behold, I fell fast asleep from just everything. From the fresh, snowy air, too. I didn't wake up until I felt Matthew take over the reins. We were in front of our house. Mama and Papa were going inside.

"Give me some of the blanket," cried Tisha. "It's cold winter out!"

Then we went for a quiet ride down the lane, just the three of us. And I told about boys and girls a hundred years from now.

"We'll be a part of the twentieth century, too!" I told them.

"We're sleighing toward 1900!" said Tisha.

"Then I will have a sleigh that *flies* through the air!" said Matthew. "Like Santa Claus — *ho!*"

The thought of it made us laugh and sing.

We stayed out in the great white night.

Finally, Matthew said, "I can't feel my hands."

"My feet are ice blocks," said Tisha.

"My ears just fell off," said I. Peals of laughter from snow-covered us.

Matthew turned the sleigh around. We grabbed hold of him as he geed-up the horses.

There, ahead of us, patches of gold made the lane sparkle. And, *ching-chinging,* we flew toward the warm lantern light of home.

Virginia Hamilton wishes to give grateful acknowledgment to Juli Overton, Coordinator of Local History, Greene County District Library, Xenia, Ohio, for her unflagging enthusiasm in this project and for her aid in uncovering pertinent historical information. Many thanks to the Xenia Branch Library, the Yellow Springs Branch Library, the Antioch College Library, and the Central State University Library — the Black Collection — for making their historical collections readily available.

The illustrations in this book were done in acrylics on D'Arches 140 lb. cold press watercolor paper.
Composition by Thompson Type, San Diego, California
Color separations by Heinz Weber, Inc., Los Angeles, California
Printed and bound by Tien Wah Press, Singapore
Production supervision by Stanley Redfern and Jan Van Gelder
Designed by Michael Farmer